BIZARRE BEINGS

Edited By Lynsey Evans

First published in Great Britain in 2024 by:

 Young**Writers**
Est. 1991 —

Young Writers
Remus House
Coltsfoot Drive
Peterborough
PE2 9BF
Telephone: 01733 890066
Website: www.youngwriters.co.uk

Printed and bound in the UK by BookPrintingUK
Website: www.bookprintinguk.com
YB0581K

FOREWORD

Welcome Reader!

Are you ready to discover weird and wonderful creatures that you'd never even dreamed of?

For Young Writers' latest competition we asked primary school pupils to create a creature of their own invention, and then write a story about it using just 100 words - a hard task! However, they rose to the challenge magnificently and the result is this fantastic collection full of creepy critters and bizarre beasts!

Here at Young Writers our aim is to encourage creativity in children and to inspire a love of the written word, so it's great to get such an amazing response, with some absolutely fantastic stories.

Not only have these young authors created imaginative and inventive creatures, they've also crafted wonderful tales to showcase their creations. These stories are brimming with inspiration and cover a wide range of themes and emotions - from fun to fear and back again!

I'd like to congratulate all the young authors in this anthology, I hope this inspires them to continue with their creative writing.

CONTENTS

Forest Glade Primary School, Sutton-In-Ashfield

Harper Jones (10)	1
Freyja Ryan-Berry (9)	2
Dylan Dixon (9)	3
Ellie-Marie Clark (9)	4
Zac Loach (9)	5
Alfie Green (10)	6
Katelyn Golds (9)	7
Pennie-Louise (9)	8
Evie Jo Curtis (9)	9
Beatrix-Anne Sills (9)	10
Lara Grace Williams (9)	11

Green End Primary School, Burnage

Bianca Hegenbarth (7)	12
Arish Alvie (8)	13
Oliver Cawley (8)	14
Sehar Fatima (8)	15
Lucas Sagüés (8)	16
Amelia Roscoe (7)	17
Ahmad Shehadeh (7)	18
Nevaeh Marriott (7)	19
Lydia Hegenbarth (7)	20

Livingstone Road Junior School, Parkstone

Tallulah Doe (8)	21
Leo Farrow (8)	22
Chloe Tanguilig (8)	23
Alex (8)	24
Samuel J Di Meglio (8)	25

Eden Taylor (8)	26
Nathan Kaznecki (9)	27
Freddie Cross (9)	28
Maya Cole (8)	29
Barney Strange (9)	30
Finley Green (8)	31
Luke Reeks (8)	32
Klay Meakin (8)	33
Thea Bryant (8)	34
Phoebe Bendall (8)	35
Hugh Gilbert (8)	36
Mason Bowley (8)	37
Grace Fletcher (9)	38
Kasen Robbie (9)	39
Adrianna Lander (9)	40
Taya Lankstead (8)	41
Jack Hustings (8)	42
Edward Palmer Bennett (9)	43
Kelly Musamba (8)	44
Millie Morris (8)	45
Ikra Almalikuyu (8)	46
Maddison Dimond (8)	47
Amari Smith (8)	48
Zuzanna Dymerska (8)	49
Stanley King (9)	50
Maria Ashley Sousa (8)	51

St Aloysius' Primary School, Chapelhall

Taylor Macaulay (9)	52
Beth Fishwick (10)	53
Shay Burns (10)	54
Jacob Robert (10)	55
Callum William Taylor (11)	56
Theo Pender (10)	57

Romeesa Zaheer (10)	58
Jack Flanigan (10)	59
Conlan Devlin (11)	60
Lucy McKinstray (9)	61
Jessica Currie (9)	62
Luke Anderson (9)	63
Anthony Dempsey (10)	64
Jack Stack (10)	65
Leah Jenkins (10)	66

The Minster School, Southwell

Pippa Barker-Runiewicz (7)	67
Maja Lee (8)	68
Polly Stendall (8)	69
Milo Ball (8)	70
Evelyn Pain (8)	71
Esther Schofield-Linnell (9)	72
Matilda Mondeschein (8)	73
Ophelia Snowden (8)	74
Nancy Kelly (7)	75
Liberty Lion (9)	76
Elodie Thomas (9)	77
Tiffany Siu (8)	78
Henry Merrix (8)	79
Evie Dawn (7)	80
Thomas Loban (9)	81
Eric Jordan (8)	82
Martha Provost (7)	83

Whirley Primary School, Macclesfield

Sophia Leon (10)	84
Samuel Mather	85
Jacob Eaton (9)	86
Sidney Smith (8)	87
Ruby Iftkhar (8)	88
Esme Cope (10)	89
Isla Hogan (10)	90
Rosa Lamptey (7)	91
Matthew W (10)	92
Millie Harrad	93
Isla Mather (8)	94

Rojvan Madiba Alagoz (10)	95
Fynn Prowting (7)	96
Eliza White (8)	97
Luke Pateman (7)	98
Beth Shaul (7)	99
Sophie Arrowsmith (9)	100
Amara Lamptey-Spencer (7)	101
Erin Tench (9)	102
Aiden Choi (7)	103
Isabelle Hibberts (11)	104
Bella Heyes (8)	105
Elijah Cockburn (7)	106
Olive McGillivray (8)	107
Bella Hill (10)	108
Gethin Herbert (9)	109
Molly Hogan (8)	110
Evie Ashcroft (7)	111
Luca West (9)	112
Flynn Simister (8)	113
Charlie Macey (8)	114
Max Handley (7)	115
Arthur Gerrard (8)	116
Ava McClelland (7)	117
Rory Owen (7)	118
Orla Hill (8)	119
Ella Scragg (8)	120
Emily Stuart (8)	121
Harry Kershaw (7)	122
Bobby Villers (7)	123
Isabelle Whitehead (10)	124
Isaac Jackson (8)	125
Isla Dougan (9)	126
Max Joseph Brown (10)	127
Ted Bailey (8)	128
Lilliana Millward (10)	129
Coen Beech (9)	130
Paddy Considine (10)	131
Harry Hibberts (9)	132
Sadie Watkins (8)	133
Nola Campbell (10)	134
Oliver Pateman (10)	135
Jude Charnock (8)	136
Eliza Utteridge (8)	137

Ellie Norbury (9)	138
Oscar Furness (11)	139
Lawrence Litherland (8)	140
Alfie Sherratt (7)	141
Eve Lewis (9)	142
Callum Casey (10)	143
Bella Burrows-Jarvis (9)	144
Lola Rowson (7)	145
Callie Davies (10)	146
Lucas Scott (11)	147
Anson Choi (10)	148
Charles Thomas (8)	149
Matilda Naughton (8)	150
Mia Scragg (10)	151
Niamh Lee (8)	152
Jack Robson (8)	153
Ronnie Tsang (9)	154
Lewis Furness (9)	155
Edwin Williams-Higuchi (10)	156
Freddie Blackburn (8)	157
Ashley Foster (10)	158
Annabel Jones (10)	159
Shea Raylance (8)	160
Poppy Barnes (9)	161
Matthew Cain (9)	162
Jacob Morton-Collings (8)	163
Lucas Olive (9)	164
Savannah Woodward (9)	165

Please read pg 72 first.

THE STORIES

Mysterious Adventures

As a girl called Libby sat on her own, she heard a mysterious sound. She peeped over and started thinking that something was off.

Libby looked again, and she couldn't believe her eyes. She saw red eyes, fangs and laser beams from behind. She couldn't believe her eyes.

The monster quickly shape-shifted and acted like nothing had happened. They told each other their names. "I'm Libby," said Libby.

"I'm Bunny," said the mysterious monster.

Libby was terrified, but Bunny looked fine.

Bunny shape-shifted again. Libby was terrified. Bunny whispered something in Libby's ear and told her to get out...

Harper Jones (10)
Forest Glade Primary School, Sutton-In-Ashfield

Stitch And Friends

Once, there was someone named Stitch. He was an amazing, fuzzy cutie and lived with his friend Lilo and her sister Nani.

People always called him ugly, but actually, they were butt-heads. Everyone hated this group too. Every single person helped them except Myrtle, she bullied people all the time. No one ever messed with them. They knew not to shout at each other at school.

At school, everyone went to the hula classes. Not this family. Only the girl's mum and dad. Now everything was hard because someone would always either forget their hula skirt or sleep in.

Freyja Ryan-Berry (9)
Forest Glade Primary School, Sutton-In-Ashfield

The Enchanted Kingdom

A boy was long lost in the middle of nowhere. He wandered until suddenly noises hit him at the top of his ear. He turned back. Nothing was there.
He kept walking until he saw mountains cascading to the clouds, high above. When he got there, the crowd went silent. Horns were echoing everywhere. The boy ran and saw an army of people behind him. He ran into a mysterious cavern he'd never imagined! Inside was destroyed from the treetops to the ground below.
The boy got catastrophically close to the edge of the cliff. Sweat rolled down his back...

Dylan Dixon (9)
Forest Glade Primary School, Sutton-In-Ashfield

Wilderwolf

Wilderwolf was bored in maths, as per usual, and noticed her fingers were growing sharp, almost like claws, and her legs were furier than a gorilla. Wilder sprinted to the bathroom, frantically calling her mother, and then... Wilderwolf almost screamed! Her mother told her she was a werewolf! Wilder now had to go to monster school, which she thought was ridiculous as she wasn't a monster.

Lula the wolf was mean. Lula had the power to make a person oblivious to what had happened. Wilder walked in nervous, not knowing who to trust. Little did she know...

Ellie-Marie Clark (9)
Forest Glade Primary School, Sutton-In-Ashfield

Lonely Zacattack

Once upon a fiery time, on a planet called Oogabooga, lived a creature with laser beams for eyes and the sharpest, scariest tail that could slice you in half in one swipe. His special gift was that he could turn himself invisible in the blink of an eye.

There was only one issue with Zacattack, he didn't have any friends. The only thing he wanted most in life was a mate. He had lots of awful, mean and nasty enemies, but never a friend. Zacattack never wanted to be alone, all he wanted was friendship. Zacattack finally met a friend.

Zac Loach (9)
Forest Glade Primary School, Sutton-In-Ashfield

Sophie And Her Mysterious Pet

Let's meet Sophie, a young ten-year-old girl with blonde curly hair and blue eyes.

There's something about her dog called Sid! Sid has a mysterious talent that Sophie has kept a secret for as long as she can remember.

Sid isn't like any other dog, he is a shape-shifter! He is always there to rescue Sophie in sticky situations. For example, he turned into a lion and chased away her bullies. Or when he turned into a bird to save her from a well.

Sophie loves him no matter how different he is to all of the other pets.

Alfie Green (10)
Forest Glade Primary School, Sutton-In-Ashfield

The Orangutan

One day, the orangutan thought it was good to fight the digger. Her home was gone and she fell. The digger was massive and the orangutan was mad, so she fought for her home and life.
One of the workers noticed the orangutan and told the digger to stop what it was doing to all of the monkeys' and birds' homes. The digger stopped and a man got out and looked at all of the deforestation he'd caused. The orangutan grabbed onto one of the workers and started swinging, but the worker picked it up and placed it somewhere safe.

Katelyn Golds (9)
Forest Glade Primary School, Sutton-In-Ashfield

The Bagpipe Badgers

The day had arisen. Today was the day the badgpipers and the fluffangs duelled. Huffle sat down in fear, not knowing her strength. All she had to do was whistle into the bagpipe, then all the fluffangs would be gone in a twist. Zing hated Huffle. Zing even tried to kill her, but after many failed attempts, gave up, as Huffle had learned her strength was more powerful than any other badgpiper. Her pipes were enchanted to protect her, as she was an orphan, and her dead angel parents wanted to keep Huffle safe and let her grow up.

Pennie-Louise (9)
Forest Glade Primary School, Sutton-In-Ashfield

The Smart Kids

Once upon a time, there was a monster whose name was Dragon, and he was really smart. The sad thing was that he had no friends. He was the smartest in the class, and that's the reason no one liked him.

One day, they had a new kid in class, his name was Fred Billy Fangs. After that day, no one liked him because he was smart too.

At lunch, the smart kids met. They had a little chat and became best friends.

Later that day, the whole class wanted to be friends, because they realised they were both aliens.

Evie Jo Curtis (9)
Forest Glade Primary School, Sutton-In-Ashfield

Untitled

On a mysterious winter morning, an unusual bird was sitting on a tree. You may think this was normal, however, this was the only odd tree out there, the rest were perfectly spread apart with beautiful, gleaming, bold leaves.

Anything that got in the bird's way was binned instantly. No one hesitated. The population was dropping like flies.

It turned out that the old man was that mysterious bird's owner. That explained why every time he walked past, he was completely fine. Long lost bird owner man...

Beatrix-Anne Sills (9)
Forest Glade Primary School, Sutton-In-Ashfield

Alien Friend

There was a creature who lived in space. One day, the creature got a name, it was Bob. To celebrate his name, Bob got a spaceship and went to Earth to make friends.

When he got there, there were lots of people that he could be friends with, but there was one person who looked lonely. Bob went to him and asked if he wanted to be friends. At first, he said no, so Bob asked again. This time he said, "Yes."

After a year of being friends, he told Bob his secret: he was an alien from outer space.

Lara Grace Williams (9)
Forest Glade Primary School, Sutton-In-Ashfield

Monsters YouTube Story

Once there was a turquoise monster named Blue.
He had powers like laser eyes, shape-shifting,
awesome flips, super speed and invisibility.
He was a happy monster but there was one thing
he didn't like. It was because he didn't have a job.
One day, one of his friends came to his house.
Their name was Greeny. When his friend came, he
was watching YouTube.
"Blue, you've been watching YouTube for over four
hours now."
"But it's so addictive!"
"How about we have a YouTube channel?"
"Okay."
So, they went to an arcade but they met a villain.
They became friends.

Bianca Hegenbarth (7)
Green End Primary School, Burnage

Friendship Forever

Garneg was lonely in the woods until he heard his favourite music.

He slowly, cautiously and carefully crept over to the place where the pleasant music was coming from and he had a peek. He saw a speaker with a face.

"I am all alone," said the speaker.

Garneg walked over and asked, "Can I be your friend?"

"Would you really be my friend?" replied Speakerhead

From that day onward, Garneg and Speakerhead became good friends. Whenever Garneg was upset, Speakerhead would play melodious songs for him.

Garneg protected Speakerhead from danger and rain so it did not shortcircuit.

Arish Alvie (8)

Green End Primary School, Burnage

The Hidden Treasure

In one tiny cupboard lived a monster called Bob, the friendliest monster you could meet. One day, Bob went to explore the wild. He found a castle and HotChilly lived there with the treasure.
Bob wanted the treasure so much that he broke in. HotChilly was hiding unnoticed in a hole. Bob didn't suspect a thing. HotChilly pounced out and Bob screamed and ran towards the treasure.
HotChilly ran to catch Bob. Bob found the treasure but HotChilly caught him.
Bob wriggled and jiggled to get out. He did, but he lost the treasure.
Bob snatched the treasure off HotChilly.

Oliver Cawley (8)
Green End Primary School, Burnage

The Adventures Of Catenkin

Once upon a time, Catenkin was just chilling in Catenkin land with Evie, Aroush, Lucas, Harry and Aizah.

They all went on an amazing flight to the UK. When they reached the UK, they saw weird aliens everywhere, but they started tackling them with their taekwondo skills, slapping every single super weird alien.

They went to their hotel but no one spoke the Catenkin language. One of the signs was in English. They learnt how to speak English because the receptionist knew both languages. So she taught them and they lived happily ever after in their cosy, nice, fluffy room.

Sehar Fatima (8)
Green End Primary School, Burnage

15

The Special Bat

Once there was a planet named The Grim. All there was on the planet were bats: Mexican bats, Greek bats, any type of bat you could imagine.

But one of the bats was special. He was called Devil. Devil was half bat, half devil. His enemy was a snake called Snape; she was a python and Devil hated pythons.

Once she visited him and he was not happy about her swallowing his friends whole. They then became enemies forever.

Snape had the power to hypnotise anyone, but not a devil, so every time she visited him, she hypnotised his friends.

Lucas Sagüés (8)

Green End Primary School, Burnage

Monsters And The Dog

Once upon a time, there was a monster who lived in a forest. He was scared of bees and giant dogs. When it was nighttime, dogs and bees came, so he hid. He was hunting for food. His cave was far away, so he couldn't get home. He had to be brave or else he wouldn't get home. He hunted the dogs and bees. He cooked them. He was so proud because he'd faced his fear.

He wasn't scared of bees and dogs anymore so he celebrated with a party with a cake, cookies and ice cream. It was fun.

Amelia Roscoe (7)
Green End Primary School, Burnage

17

Ralph And The Great Fire

Once upon a time, there was a great fire that kept a ninja village warm. One day, a seven-headed dog took the fire out. So Ralph, a professional ninja kid, went on an adventure to get the help of a legendary great wizard that lives on a big mountain.

After days of travelling, he finally asked the wizard for help and when they arrived to the village, the dog was waiting, but the wizard scared the seven-headed dog with a rumbling huge storm and then lit the fire back on with his magic.

Ahmad Shehadeh (7)

Green End Primary School, Burnage

The Curse Of Scotybot

Firstly, Scotybot was under a bed practising his magic skills and heard the people talking. So he popped his head out.

He heard them say that they were going under the bed because they needed the beachboard because they were going to the beach.

He thought he would curse them so they came and were cursed. The curse he did was for them to be frozen for a year.

Nevaeh Marriott (7)
Green End Primary School, Burnage

19

The Monster Made A Family

Once there was a cute monster. He was infinitely cute when he ate snacks.

One day a family came near him. They knew that he was crazy about sweets, so they gave him a Hubba Bubba. He ate it in one go and they laughed. The monster hugged them and they hugged him back.

By the way, his name was Bubblegum.

Lydia Hegenbarth (7)
Green End Primary School, Burnage

Something Sad

In the middle of London sits a little girl crying.
There is a big bang... She looks up.
"Hello," a green alien says, wiggling his arms.
The little girl giggles as she looks at his
heterochromia eyes.
"Hi," she says.
"Slun," the alien says, trying to say his name.
He jiggles his arms and legs again.
"Friends?" Slun asks.
"Friends," the girl responds, happily.
They walk off into the sunset, laughing and smiling.
Therefore, from that day, Little May, for that was
her name, has never cried or whined again, just
happiness and laughter.
"Ha, ha, ha!"

Tallulah Doe (8)
Livingstone Road Junior School, Parkstone

The Journey To Much Disaster!

The day of sending a man to Mars had come! "T-minus ten... one, blast off!"
Fast forward five days. As the astronaut, who called himself Juggernaut, was cooking some rations, control called him. "Juggernaut, five days left of living in a rocket!"
Juggernaut replied, "Yeah, feeling fine. Ready to be the first person to land on Mars."
Fast forward to the landing. "Time to take the first step on Mars." Juggernaut took his first step on Mars. He started taking a walk down the side of Mars but as he was walking he got bitten but killed the bug immediately...

Leo Farrow (8)

Livingstone Road Junior School, Parkstone

The Crazy Awesome Adventure!

On Evil Land, there lived two aliens called Bob and Gobble. Their skills were eating, teleporting and shooting bricks, and they'd been BFFs since pre-school.

They were bored and wanted to leave the class. An angel came and got inside their bodies. They were nice to their coach, even though they had to be evil.

The two got detention and they were nice and didn't mind.

"Please shoot us for proof!" they both said.

"Okay, guys!" said Mr Evil, and he shot them.

"OMG, you're back," cried Mr Evil. "I think the nice angel got in your bodies!"

Chloe Tanguilig (8)

Livingstone Road Junior School, Parkstone

The Golden Slayer And The Villain

Once upon a time, there was a creature called Golden Slayer. He used to live in outer space, but then the gravity source was broken!

The spaceship's glass broke. The only way for him to get out was to jump out!

While he was sleeping, he woke up to see that his spaceship was destroyed. Then, he started dying.

After a while, he landed on Earth, but then out of nowhere a villain appeared!

Golden Slayer didn't run, he just asked one thing, "Do you know where my mum and dad are?"

He said, "No."

After a year they trained.

Alex (8)
Livingstone Road Junior School, Parkstone

The Abominable Revenge Of King Pen!

On Planet Comic lived two aliens called Jamie and XOYZ; they were best friends since they were born. Meanwhile, on Planet Skull, evil King Pen and Queen Rubber found an advertisement that said if they destroyed a planet, they would win 9,999,999 billion dollars! They decided to demolish Planet Comic!
Meanwhile, on Planet Comic, Jamie saw the news and knew what was going to happen! He quickly galloped to XOYZ's apartment to tell him about this! Together they made a spaceship with a death ray. So they shot the death ray and hit the baddies. Yay! At last, victory!

Samuel J Di Meglio (8)
Livingstone Road Junior School, Parkstone

Untitled

In Planet Coboo, there is a monster called Happy Slappy. He is always happy, but one day, something happens. Slappy is quite slimy, and on top of his head, he has a pipe that can shoot slime. He can also fly around.

Slappy wakes up one morning and sees a rocket coming down from the sky onto the planet. "Evacuate," shouts Slappy.

It is Horrified Harry, the leader of the bad gang. Everyone runs into their homes, but Slappy stands there, ready to fight. He shoots slime into Harry's eyes. Harry falls off the planet. He did it!

Eden Taylor (8)
Livingstone Road Junior School, Parkstone

A Blue Chicken

Once a chicken time ago, a chicken was killing Cyclops Chickens in space, but the Cyclops Chickens made a Cyclops Chicken spaceship and made the Venom Chicken run into the darkness. The Venom Chicken was mean and broke out of prison in the Cyclops Chicken spaceship. The Cyclops Chickens were made to get him. Venom Chicken had too much. He was now using venom stuff, which poisons Cyclops Chickens, but it was too much. The Cyclops Chickens won the battle, and they were happy that they won the battle. Venom Chicken was locked up in Cyclops prison.

Nathan Kaznecki (9)
Livingstone Road Junior School, Parkstone

Robot Oobleek

Once, in the big land of Planet Zarg, lived a big robot called Oobleek. Oobleek was a robot, an evil robot. He'd always be up to something.

Then, one day, his enemy, Splinter, came back after 1,000 years! Splinter had big spikes on his back and on his head. Oobleek went high in the sky with his titanium wings to battle Splinter.

Finally, it'd finished. The battle was over, and Oobleek went on to always fight more crime. Splinter was gone, and so the battle was really over because nobody found him, and he was never seen again.

Freddie Cross (9)
Livingstone Road Junior School, Parkstone

Enemies Attack

In the middle of the night, in the garden of a little girl, a stinky smell started! Morning rose as the sun shimmered brightly on the golden sand of Planet Earth. As night lifted on Planet Rough, the spaceship arrived, and the gang came back. Clan said, "Hello, dear citizens," as he shape-shifted all around.

Then on Planet Earth, they now knew what the smell was—it was a special alien jelly. Clan didn't try to hurt them; he was giving them a gift for not harming Clan's Planet Earth. Good job, aliens!

Maya Cole (8)
Livingstone Road Junior School, Parkstone

29

The Space Cat Story

Once, I was stuck in Spanish class, and a huge *thump* broke the silence! When the lesson was over, Leo, Kyle, Elvis and I went to search for the noise.

"We found a space cat!" we exclaimed. The cat had an enemy called Lord Cat Fod, so we set off in a space shuttle and went to Princot.

We found him, battled with the evil cat lord and won, and Princot was freed. The space cat gave us free tickets for his planet and fifty years of luck. We said, "Bye, be back soon," and we left planet Princot.

Barney Strange (9)
Livingstone Road Junior School, Parkstone

The Disaster On Planet Oooz 2000

First, it was a normal day. All the kids were running around, splashing around, having fun. But then they heard something unusual.

Only the old monsters recognised the sound. Suddenly, it shot up and landed. Everybody evacuated, except for Gun Laser Shooter. He knew exactly who it was. It was Project Zero.

First, he sent his minions, but that was not enough. Then, he got knocked down, so he used his lasers, but that didn't work. His guns shot and still didn't work, so he used Fire Dragon Ultra Edition...

Finley Green (8)
Livingstone Road Junior School, Parkstone

Bob The Naughty Yeti

Bob the Yeti was unstoppable and destroyed everything in his path. He died in water, but his eyes were high-powered laser beams, tearing hay bales into ant-sized ashes. When humans saw Bob, they immediately knew they needed to run and hide. The people were savages; they didn't save their pet dogs or cats. Men have to, but they're too scared.

One day, John came and pushed Bob into the water. Bob woke up furious; he was locked up in a little box with scientists looking at Bob. They found out Bob was a robot.

Luke Reeks (8)
Livingstone Road Junior School, Parkstone

Road Vs Cars

Once upon a time, there was a mighty road called Worstroad, and he hated cars, especially Roy, the Bugatti. He was so fast that Worstroad couldn't come close to chomping on him. Worstroad couldn't even think that fast. He drove around and around all day long and Roy was so fast that fire was behind him. Worstroad got so mad, he just kept the road closed forever.

So, Roy made a ramp, and he went over him. Worstroad was so mad he ate the ramp, it looked like crumbs everywhere. Roy screeched to a stop.

Klay Meakin (8)
Livingstone Road Junior School, Parkstone

All About A Spiky Monster

Once upon a time, there lived a monster named Spikes, and he lived all by himself on Planet Heart. He went to school, and everyone made fun of him, so he was always upset. Nobody knew about it. This is what Spikes looked like: Spikes had three eyes and was hairy, naughty and very stinky. He smelled like homemade strawberries, only just out of the greenhouse. You would never want to see him because he was very scary-looking. If anyone spooked him, there would be snakes coming out of his fur. He was a dragon!

Thea Bryant (8)
Livingstone Road Junior School, Parkstone

The Easy Day

In school, Bob was learning how to scare a child. Miss Boo said to Bob and his friends, "Go and scare a child, but you have to take a photo." So off they went.

But as soon as Bob got there, Zip, Pip and Dip started chasing him. Then Bob threw them with his mind.

When he got there he hid under the bed. At first, he was quiet, but then he started scraping the bed. The child woke up, then Bob jumped out and took the photo, ran and went to school.

Miss Boo said, "Well done."

Phoebe Bendall (8)
Livingstone Road Junior School, Parkstone

A Mythical Beast

Once upon a time, there was a sensational beast known as The Elemental Beast. It was water, wind, earth and fire. It was magnificent and very kind. If someone called it, it would be there in a minute. It went into the woods and then saw a weird bird known as the dodo bird. It couldn't be described, but it engaged in a magnificent and dangerous fight with the beast. It used fire on the bird, but the bird survived. So, it used wind and blew the bird into the air, and the dodo bird went extinct.

Hugh Gilbert (8)

Livingstone Road Junior School, Parkstone

The Super Alien

Once upon a time, a nice, talented alien came to Earth and his name was Waldo, the nightmare fighter and robber fighter. One of the robbers he hates is called Robert. He is a very naughty criminal who has been wanted for most of his life. One night, he came to Oakshon in the middle of the night, trying to break into a little boy's house. But just in time, Waldo came to save the day. Waldo battled Robert and saved the boy from being left with no roof over his head, stopping Robert in his tracks.

Mason Bowley (8)
Livingstone Road Junior School, Parkstone

Crazy Queen

In Crazy Land, there lived things, and they were colourful, but there was a thing that was grey, and her name was Lizzy. She got teased by her family, and she had enough, so she ran away. However, she stumbled into The Queen, and she was grey too.

The Queen said, "You are my daughter."

Lizzy was shocked. Then, The Queen saw that Lizzy was cold and got her a blanket, and they went home. The Queen ran a bath, and Lizzy watched TV. When they were both done, the worst thing happened...

Grace Fletcher (9)

Livingstone Road Junior School, Parkstone

Light And Dark

It was 5:59am, one minute till light! Dark was scared; Light always hated Dark. Light was brighter, lighter and stronger. Dark couldn't do anything except hide under the bed, scared and frightened. It worked; Light didn't find him under the bed of Tom Joy, but he didn't wake up because Dark made it darker.

Dark felt so bad that he went into the light so Tom Joy would wake up for breakfast and go to school to learn. Dark always remembered to take turns being Dark and being Light!

Kasen Robbie (9)

Livingstone Road Junior School, Parkstone

Gobidie Do

Once upon a time, there lived a monster called Gobidie Do and he had one eye, long flappy ears and extra toes and fingers. Gobidie Do was starting to get hungry and at the last minute he found a little girl and he tried to snatch her but she turned and walked away. So Gobidie Do fell on the floor and he got very mad and used his teleporting powers to turn up in front of the girl, but she was actually a superhero and punched him. Then Gobidie Do flew across the world and the little girl won.

Adrianna Lander (9)
Livingstone Road Junior School, Parkstone

The Big Bad Dog

Once, there were two monsters. One was named Dragon, and the other was named Meow. However, there was a bad one named The Dog. Meow was watching The Dog, but Dragon did not know that. Then Meow went to the good side. The Dog fought Dragon, and Dragon won. Meow was in a hotel, and then The Dog turned nice. The Dog became friends with Dragon, and they had lots of fun. They went to help a lot of monsters, but one day, they got so lost that they called for help, and they found their way home.

Taya Lankstead (8)
Livingstone Road Junior School, Parkstone

Sneeker's Revenge

In the middle of a crater, there lived Sneeker, the terrifying monster, and his enemy, F. F tried to trap and kidnap him, but every night, Sneeker got stronger.

Then, F hid under the bed, and when Sneeker jumped, they got into a massive fight. F went and flew his jet but, in reality, F was sleeping. Sneeker bent the titanium, ran to the window, grabbed a parachute and jumped out, gliding to safety.

When F got up, he screamed and said, "I will get you, Sneeker."

Jack Hustings (8)

Livingstone Road Junior School, Parkstone

Bottle Bunny

Once upon a time, there was a war that lasted five whole years. This got the place as the worst war ever. Swords clashing and shields smashing, when the bunnies woke up, they had the biggest day of their whole lives. They were going to go to war. They got to put on their mum's special soap on their fluffy ears and skinny legs and then ran as fast as they could to get to the military. The military was as big as a dragon, not as small as a bunny, and then they opened the door.

Edward Palmer Bennett (9)
Livingstone Road Junior School, Parkstone

Lepade

Once upon a time, there was a creature called Mega. He was a boy. Then there was a fox called Hairy. It was a boy, a pretty crazy creature. One day, Mega was going to buy some vegetables like covo, but he was attacked by a fox. Then he was like, "Oh no, don't touch me!"
"Never ever, you will never get away!"
Mega and Hairy reached the den, and Hairy settled down and started to eat Mega. It was so bad; his mother started to look for him...

Kelly Musamba (8)
Livingstone Road Junior School, Parkstone

Golden Dragon

In a planet of dragons lived a dragon called Zogow and Minow, but one of them was golden, and that one was Minow. This made everyone want to take him; it made the royal family want him even more. The king and queen made their family leave so they would have a better chance. The royal family took Minow and Zogow, but they knew they were no match for them.

They defeated the king and queen with hope and courage. The two dragons made them regret everything that happened.

Millie Morris (8)
Livingstone Road Junior School, Parkstone

Bob Gets Kidnapped

In the middle of the invisible mountain lived Bob. He was playing with his friend in the morning. After a day, his enemy came and kidnapped him. His friend and his family were very worried about him. His friend went to look for him.

After a while, his enemy saw him, and Bob's friend started to hide. One hour later, Bob's enemy slept. Then Bob's friend found Bob, and they went home. But they didn't notice Bob's enemy was following them...

Ikra Almalikuyu (8)
Livingstone Road Junior School, Parkstone

Alytyam Vs Frica Battle

Once there were two enemies, Frica and Alytyam. They were from Planet Fricy. Alytyam helped us, but Frica hurt us.

Alytyam came to Earth and saw Frica. They battled for a while. They both stopped for a breath. Alytyam hit Frica on the head as he flew across the road.

Eventually, Frica was locked up in jail. Alytyam lived a happy, exciting life and he had a loving family. He lived a long life, but only time will tell. Will he have to take action?

Maddison Dimond (8)

Livingstone Road Junior School, Parkstone

Giant

Once upon a time, there was a giant that was trying to get the five giants, but the five giants were running away from the other giants when they could run away. So they decided not to run so they couldn't hurt them. They wanted to run away from them, but they decided not to run.

They didn't get hurt, luckily, so they went to their den to not get hurt. The giants were under the scary bed of laser beams, and the den was invisible.

Amari Smith (8)
Livingstone Road Junior School, Parkstone

Untitled

Once upon a time in Mouga, there was a creature called Goowee Boowee, and he had the force. He had turned into a creature. So when he went to a disco party, he saw his worst enemy, which was called Demy. They didn't like each other because Demy once elbowed one of Goowee's friends. So, when he said stop to Demy, he did it to a weirdo, and Goowee Boowee started to cry. Demy said, "Sorry," but they still weren't friends.

Zuzanna Dymerska (8)
Livingstone Road Junior School, Parkstone

Dragon Battle

On Planet Spot lived a monster called Eyes. One day, he was peacefully sleeping when he heard a *bang*.

Eyes went out to check, and he saw a dragon burning down Planet Spot. Eyes decided to try to kill the dragon to save the planet.

In the end, the dragon went to where he had come from. For now, Planet Spot was safe. For now...

Stanley King (9)

Livingstone Road Junior School, Parkstone

The Evil Dragon And The Good Creatures

The evil dragon was trying to destroy the Earth, but the good Shape Shifter was determined to improve the Earth. However, the dragon was invisible from the day he wanted to get revenge. So, he assembled an army to defeat the shape-shifters, but the shape-shifters managed to defeat the dragon...

Maria Ashley Sousa (8)
Livingstone Road Junior School, Parkstone

Dotty Saved The Day Again!

In Squishmallow Land, lived a squishmallow called Dotty.

Dotty had a mission to fly down to Earth. She lived up in the sky but all her missions were on Earth. There was a big monster trying to kidnap everyone. When Dotty got to Earth to stop the monster there was something unusual. There was a squishmallow like Dotty called Stripes. When she flew, her wings glowed and her stripes turned a different colour.

Their eyes were both like the sea, but Dotty's eyes glowed and Stripes' eyes froze bad guys.

Dotty had a feeling they were long lost...

Taylor Macaulay (9)
St Aloysius' Primary School, Chapelhall

Speedy The Snail

A little snail ran in and shouted, "Speedy!"
The big spotted snail said, "What's wrong?"
The little snail said, "There is a guy from Earth killing our kind."
Speedy ran so fast he was on Earth in less than 1 millisecond! Speedy ran to Lilly's house and saw a little girl and her dad.
"Dad, stop!" she said.
"They are eating our plants, Lilly!"
Speedy ran so fast he saved all the snails. Lilly liked Speedy and Speedy liked Lilly. She wanted to keep him as a pet, and Speedy agreed.

Beth Fishwick (10)
St Aloysius' Primary School, Chapelhall

The Bear Who Doesn't Care

On Planet Bebababoo, Ben The Bear who didn't care was friends with all bears, but with people or animals, he didn't care.

One day he was in his house minding his own business when lots of kids were robbing his house. He used his massive hand and punched the kids away.

The next day, police came and arrested him. He was devastated. He'd been arrested for being a monstrosity to other people and got ten months in jail.

In jail, he was bullied by animals and humans. He was the only bear.

He punched the ground and broke himself out.

Shay Burns (10)
St Aloysius' Primary School, Chapelhall

Untitled

Snail With A Tail was slugging around New York when his snail sense went off.
A snail was robbing a shop. Jeff used his jetpack and flew to help. He shot gooey webs at him. He became Snail in Jail!
Jeff's snail sense went again. Another robbery! He used his jetpack and landed on the robber who tried to hit Jeff but failed!
Jeff spat hot water at the robber. A spider bit Jeff and he duplicated himself.
He said, "Duplicate, you stay here."
The boss snail was robbing the bank. Jeff saved the day and defeated them *all*!

Jacob Robert (10)
St Aloysius' Primary School, Chapelhall

Rocky And The Space Rocks

Rocky the monster searched for space rocks. He needed them to fuel his spaceship which had landed on Earth. Rocky was from Jupiter and was desperate to get home. Meteors from Jupiter hit Earth. He was searching for them to power his ship when he came across Callum, a human from Earth. Callum helped Rocky to search for fuel and taught him how humans lived on Earth.

By the time Rocky and Callum found the fuel they realised many differences between both planets. However, this only made their friendship stronger. They agreed to visit each other every year...

Callum William Taylor (11)
St Aloysius' Primary School, Chapelhall

Bob The Monkey Alien

Bob The Monkey Alien lived on Banana Planet. But there was one problem: he had run out of holy bananas!

He went on his monkey spaceship to Earth to find some. He needed them to continue living on Banana Planet.

He landed in a cave. Inside, he came across some gorillas. He tried many of their rotten bananas but they didn't work.

He became friends with the other gorillas because they wanted to help him find a holy banana.

They found one and he ate it—all of his superpowers were regained, so he could go back to Banana Planet.

Theo Pender (10)
St Aloysius' Primary School, Chapelhall

Untitled

A girl called Maya is strong, nice, powerful and calm. Her superpower was invisibility and she could control the weather too. Maya was on a mission. Maya was going to go to Palestine to help the people by using her powers. Maya heard that Israel was launching bombs and grenades at Palestine and houses were getting damaged causing deaths. Maya went in the aeroplane where she saw a lot of bombs being launched from Israel. Maya arrived in Palestine and saw a lot of houses damaged. Then Maya brought food for the people. They were so thankful for food.

Romeesa Zaheer (10)
St Aloysius' Primary School, Chapelhall

Superdog Saves Tucker

One day in Dogsglow there was a dog named Max. He wasn't a normal dog, he had superpowers. He was just chilling until he got an alert that a cat named Tucker was getting attacked in Chapelhall Woods by a fox. So he got in his universe travel machine. Superdog was now at Chapelhall Woods. Tucker said, "Who are you?"

Superdog said, "I am Superdog and I am here to save you from that fox."

Tucker said, "Thank you!" Superdog got him away from the fox. Then both of them became best friends.

Jack Flanigan (10)
St Aloysius' Primary School, Chapelhall

Mike Tyson Saves The Day

Conlan and Jacob were walking and saw a haunted cabin, so they went and explored. It was a really big house with tall stairs and boarded windows. They went to walk out but a monster jumped out and kidnapped Jacob.

Conlan ran away and did not come back. Conlan had nothing except one special idea, to phone a very, very popular friend who would be stronger than the monster, Mike Tyson. He flew all the way to Scotland and went with Conlan. They got in the cabin and Mike one-punched the monster, and they saved the day.

Conlan Devlin (11)
St Aloysius' Primary School, Chapelhall

Under The Sea

One day in the sea land, under the water it was really bright and sunny. There was a whale called Bob. Bob had no friends, it was awful. Bob liked to wear bows but the older people in the sea bullied him and it wasn't fair. He had no confidence. Then a pink narwhal swam in and said, "Stop bullying him, it's not fair!" He'd done this because he was celebrating sea creatures who have different appearances. Bob was so happy when the narwhal said this, but the sea creatures still bullied him.

Lucy McKinstray (9)
St Aloysius' Primary School, Chapelhall

The Alien Who Wanted Friends

Bob the Alien Bear was on a mission to get friends. Five hundred years ago, he had lived in a school. One day, he burst into class and asked, "Can anyone be my friend?"

But everyone was scared of him, so they said no. He lay down in his bed wondering why everyone was so scared of him. He became sad and angry so he burst into the classroom and grabbed a desk and threw it.

Then, the class felt so bad and asked him if he wanted to be their friend.

He was so happy he had friends...

Jessica Currie (9)
St Aloysius' Primary School, Chapelhall

The Cyborg's Mission

Once upon a time, there was a robot named Mark. He had a big job protecting everyone on Earth from asteroids. It was a hard job because if he was late for a mission it was most likely that everyone would die.

This was a different mission for Mark. A hard one! On Mars, he noticed a massive metal building. He told his flying wolves to sniff the place. He placed a bomb and told his wolves, "Behind me," and he blew it up! The four asteroids were already heading for Earth. Was Mark too late?

Luke Anderson (9)
St Aloysius' Primary School, Chapelhall

A Friend For A Spiky Monster

Bob the big spiky was dark blue with pink dashes on his skin. He had eight eyes, long arms, spikes for fingers and a spiky head. He looked really scary and the problem was all he wanted was to make friends but everyone would run away. He tried so many times but he decided to try one more time. He went into a big crowd of people but they all ran away, but one kid stayed and wanted to be friends, so they both became best friends.

Anthony Dempsey (10)
St Aloysius' Primary School, Chapelhall

Monster Woods

Jim the monster had blue spiky hair with bright yellow dashes. One night the monster was in his shed sleeping in the haunted woods.
Conlan and Jack went for a walk through the woods where they came across Jim's house. Jack and Conlan went into the monster's house. He kidnapped both of them but Conlan escaped and he tried to get Jack to safety. Conlan managed to sneak into the shed and rescue Jack.

Jack Stack (10)
St Aloysius' Primary School, Chapelhall

Maxa The Crazy But Kind Creature

Once upon a time, there was a little creature called Maxa. She had a big job. Maxa wanted to save the country she lived in. Maxa was a very crazy but kind creature. She always wanted to help and work in a job but everyone thought she was too crazy. She just wanted to help.

Now that she had calmed down a bit, she worked to help the country she lived in. Maxa was so happy and helpful, and calm now.

Leah Jenkins (10)
St Aloysius' Primary School, Chapelhall

Blobby Makes New Friends

Once, there was a monster called Blobby. He loved the red squirrels and enjoyed playing with them. But he chased the grey squirrels that invaded Britain.

One day, Blobby got stuck on some very sticky fungus. A couple of grey squirrels laughed and mocked him. "*Haha!* You're stuck!" Blobby felt very sad.

A baby squirrel from that family felt sorry for Blobby. He asked, "Are you okay?" He helped Blobby get off the fungus.

Blobby thought, *maybe grey squirrels are okay after all!* They began to play, and Blobby became friends with the grey squirrels. He never chased them again.

Pippa Barker-Runiewicz (7)

The Minster School, Southwell

A Strong Friendship

Once upon a time, a little girl got told off for doing a question wrong. "That question is wrong, you get detention!"

"Wait, it was only one."

After school, she came home crying. Eventually, she calmed down and asked her mum if she could go to the park. Her mother said, "Yes."

When she got to the park, bones started to fall down like snowflakes. "An alien, an alien!" people shouted.

"I am King Bony, I come in peace. I have come to live with Lilly." King Bony supported her with her maths. "I will not leave, you're my friend!"

Maja Lee (8)
The Minster School, Southwell

Fight From Maroog To Earth

Bob couldn't believe it. His old enemy had come to Earth! They fought for ages and people started to tell stories about Bob, like, "Have you heard there's a monster about?" This one was told by one of a child's friends, but she disagreed. *Maybe he's nice*, wondered the girl.

That night she set off looking for the creature and soon she found it. An animal that seemed to be fighting a *real* monster. So the girl dashed home to get her dad's net and caught the real monster. Then she went over to Bob and stroked his soft feathers.

Polly Stendall (8)
The Minster School, Southwell

69

The Ocean Monster

Lurking in the ocean you will find this monstrous beast. All life in the sea fears this thing. It uses the currents to move from place to place, engulfing everything that gets in the way. Immense in size, it's slimy, smelly and very dangerous. But it might not be what you think.
It's not a great white shark with razor-sharp teeth. It's not a colossal squid with deadly tentacles. Oh no! This monster's a crime against the environment and lives for hundreds of years. This monster is the Great Pacific Garbage Patch. The most dangerous monster in the ocean.

Milo Ball (8)
The Minster School, Southwell

Spoodle's Story

This is Spoodle. He is my small, crazy, funny creature. Spoodle has a problem. His enemies, The Tiks from Tikadoodle Land, are making him sad. It was Spoodle's first day of Monster School. He was in the playground when The Tiks landed their spaceship right in front of him. They got out and spat at Spoodle. From that moment he knew they were enemies! What The Tiks didn't know was that Spoodle had special powers! "Jellyeos Zarmosh!" The Tiks were turned to jelly. The Queen of Pita Pata Land awarded Spoodle a medal and asked him to share his story.

Evelyn Pain (8)
The Minster School, Southwell

The Mixed Up Monster

Once there was a monster that wanted some friends but no one liked her because she wasn't scary. She was out once and she hid behind a curtain because she saw another monster. Suddenly, she heard a great big *bang!* It was only the pipes, but she didn't know! She jumped out, running away, and terrified the other monsters. They ran up to her. They said, "You scared us so much you can come and live with us."
"Thank you," she said. "What shall we play?"
They played tag and sardines and she lived happily ever after.

Esther Schofield-Linnell (9)
The Minster School, Southwell

Dave The Dragon Saves The Day!

One day on Monster Island, Dave the Dragon heard something in the night. A scream, followed by, "Shh" and then silence. Immediately, Dave knew what it was. Devon the Demon had kidnapped someone, but who? Dave called his friend, Bob the Alien, but no answer.

When Dave went outside there were missing posters for Bob. Dave immediately made a plan to save him. His plan was to go to Devon's cave and breathe fire at him to make him run away.

When he got there, he signalled to Bob to distract Devon. Dave then breathed fire and scared Devon away.

Matilda Mondeschein (8)
The Minster School, Southwell

Gizmo's Good Turn

On Planet Gloop there lived a little fluffy creature called Gizmo. Gizmo loved to read. She read morning, noon and night and spent most of her free time in the library.

One day she decided to go to the National History Museum on Planet Earth. She had heard all about it on Gloop News. When Gizmo arrived at the museum, she saw someone struggling to read a sign. She went over to help. They became friends and explored the exhibitions together, learning all about animals and dinosaurs.

Gizmo went home feeling very happy that she had helped someone in need.

Ophelia Snowden (8)
The Minster School, Southwell

Violet Tooksbry

Violet Tooksbry lived in Crazy Town. She could destroy nightmares and she could shoot out ice balls. Her enemy was Wolf Scar, he appeared when there was a full moon. He had bright yellow eyes and razor-sharp teeth.

One full moon, Wolf Scar sucked little boys' and girls' nice dreams out and replaced them with nightmares. Violet stopped him by destroying the nightmares. She shot out ice balls at Wolf Scar and turned him into a block of ice. What a nightmare for him. Then Violet's head fell off. Everyone in Crazy Town was in a nightmare!

Nancy Kelly (7)
The Minster School, Southwell

Lost But Found

There was a sudden *boom* as Scarlet got sent to Earth without her parents, as an invasion was happening. Once she had landed on Earth, she met some farm animals and they soon became friends. But as she'd landed, the farmer called the police and pest control to come and get her. The friends managed to get out of their enclosure and promised to build a shuttle to get her home. Once they lost the police trail, they promised to start building the shuttle. It was hard but once it was done she said goodbye to her friends and left.

Liberty Lion (9)
The Minster School, Southwell

Dolphin Demon's Adventure

One day, when Dolphin Demon was at school, the teacher announced that there was a new underwater animal in the class. The next day, Dolphin Demon and Jealous Jellyfish got to know each other a lot better (they played with each other too). Dolphin Demon's favourite class was next, maths. He was so smart he got every question correct. Jealous Jellyfish was so jealous, and after he was so mean to Dolphin Demon. (Dolphin Demon is supposed to be the mean one and Jealous Jellyfish the kind one.) They swapped sides and Dolphin Demon is good now.

Elodie Thomas (9)
The Minster School, Southwell

Linth

NASA has a new task for Dr Smith, to go to Jupiter with his newly invented gun. When he arrives he performs experiments on his gun, which shoots out giant bubbles.

Suddenly, a girl comes out and jumps into a giant bubble. She transforms into a new creature; Dr Smith names it Linth. Linth has half a red side and half black. It has three powerful laser eyes and they shoot out laser beams. Linth can fly with two wings and its tail has power.

Dr Smith catches Linth and brings it back to the Earth for further investigation.

Tiffany Siu (8)
The Minster School, Southwell

Thirsty Brutus

Once, in the middle of a football match, a young boy called Brutus was so thirsty, when he took a shot he missed the whole goal! The other players were extremely disappointed with him. However, Juicy the Juice Tank was watching the match and with that, he juiced himself to Earth and got to the boy in the nick of time. Juicy blasted the boy in the mouth with apple juice. With that, Brutus had lots of energy, zoomed back onto the pitch and scored the winning goal. He was awarded Player of the Match and everyone cheered.

Henry Merrix (8)
The Minster School, Southwell

Cats Vs Witches

Once, there was a small pink cat that had glow-in-the-dark hearts and a marshmallow on its head. When Catmallow was on the way to school with her human friend, they took a wrong turn and came to an old, spooky house. Catmallow told the girl not to look in the window, but she did! When she looked inside, she saw a witch, and they heard the witch's evil plan to take over the world. Luckily, Catmallow knew how to catch mice, so they used a really big mouse catcher to trap the witch, and that saved everyone.

Evie Dawn (7)
The Minster School, Southwell

Zabada

Here in Zackudack 374, the loneliest planet in the galaxy, there is one alien race like no other. His name is Zaplan. He has many abilities like floating, has the force, uses lightning and breathes in space. He is the most popular alien in the galaxy, everybody knows him. Sometimes he can be a bit mischievous. Stopping people up to no good, Zaplan tries to stop them by using his powers. His arch nemesis is Trara the Devil of the underworld. Zaplan's friends, Zela, Leica, Cara and Zemla, all defend him.

Thomas Loban (9)
The Minster School, Southwell

The Tale Of The Taco Trickster

One day there was a taco whose name was
Triangle Trickster. The naughty Triangle Trickster
played an unkind trick on the nice guacamole. The
taco had stirred in tomato salsa, which got very
messy. Next, the Triangle Trickster scooped up
some grated cheese and cheekily threw it.
The Taco Trickster came to a sticky end because
Mum covered it in jalapeños and ate it.

Eric Jordan (8)
The Minster School, Southwell

A Friend For Lilly

Once there was a creature called Lilly. Her planet blew up and she never knew. She came home but it was gone. She was all alone and very scared. She flew to a different planet and hit the earth in the shape-shifted form of a dot. She found new friends and family. She now lives with them.

Martha Provost (7)
The Minster School, Southwell

Cherry

At her odd home, Nauphalophagous, Bloopie sat on the fluffy grass staring at her mechanical heart. She longed for more adventure, fear and frights. In the corner of her eye was a crimson red fruit labelled 'Cherry. From Earth'.

She knew what to do. Thus, she used the warp crystals forbidden to her kind.

"So, this is Earth," muttered Bloopie. "Strange place," she whispered. It was an archaeological site.

"What's that?" hollered the people. Humans. Loads of humans, staring. Questions sprouted up everywhere, and confusion spread like wildfire. Humans. Coming back home, her family jumped with joy. Home again. Home.

Sophia Leon (10)
Whirley Primary School, Macclesfield

Scrambled

One day Samuel walked to school. Suddenly there stood his enemy Mia Scrambled Egg. Without hesitation, he closed his eyes and said, "Ding dong doodle doo," and a mysterious crazy creature appeared.

Samuel opened his eyes. "Hi, Ding Dong Donkey! I don't know what to do, it's Mia Scrambled Egg. I need help," said Samuel.

"Okay," said Ding Dong Donkey. "Don't let her bother you. Don't let anyone bother you. Tell your teacher or parent, they can always help you. Continue your walk to school and try to ignore her."

"Goodbye then," said Samuel.

"Goodbye."

Samuel Mather
Whirley Primary School, Macclesfield

YoungWriters Est. 1991

A Reek No More

At lunchtime, in St Maria's School, a disgusting, putrid reek came from the cafeteria. Broccoli and chicken! Bonnie was seven and lunch was her least favourite time in school. Luckily, she thought it was not like tortoise snot porridge!

Before she tucked in... *Whoosh! Bang!* Surprisingly, a black hole appeared above her and a weird creature fell out. "Hi, I'm Lhomfh." Suddenly, its eyes grew and Bonnie spotted it was staring at her food. Before she knew it, Lhomfh had bounced onto the table and it was delighted! Lhomfh demolished everything but suddenly... *Kablam!* It had exploded... the broccoli...

Jacob Eaton (9)
Whirley Primary School, Macclesfield

The Best Roller Coaster In The World

On Ugabar lived a friendly monster named Zaygon with his sidekick Sweepertentacle, a purple blob with yellow tentacles.

On Zaygon's birthday, Sweepertentacle surprised him with a trip to a funfair. They headed towards the roller coaster but when they were on it the ground started rumbling. It was the evil Thundercracker, he was ready to destroy the best roller coaster in the galaxy. Everyone was petrified. Sweepertentacle jumped on his drone and whizzed around Thundercracker at the speed of light, making him really dizzy. Zaygon saw his chance and grabbed his golden axe and destroyed Thundercracker with a single blow.

Sidney Smith (8)
Whirley Primary School, Macclesfield

Fearless

Running, scared, surrounded by towering, emerald trees, hearing branches crunch under her feet as she trembled through the damp, misty forest.
Isobel thought of being bullied by three mean girls. They kept embarrassing her by telling Isobel's friends her personal information. This made her disheartened.
All of a sudden, *bang!* Isobel bumped into a... thing!
"Who, or, what are you?" Isobel asked, puzzled.
"Hi, I am the creature of your imagination. I am fearless. Go back and stand up to those mean girls!"
Later that day, she did. She did it! All because of that little creature.

Ruby Iftkhar (8)
Whirley Primary School, Macclesfield

Lolly Sugarush Saves The Day

Lolly Sugarush was preparing for the junior Sherbet Slope skiing competition. She was the head judge and was making sure the surface was smooth with no lumps or bumps. The Candykids taking part chattered excitedly, waiting for their turn skiing.

Suddenly, the evil Candycrusher came barrelling down the mountain towards them like a huge cannonball. He was going to smash the Candykids like skittles! Without thinking, Lolly grabbed her big candy cane like a hockey stick and gave chase. *Thwack!* She hit the Candycrusher so hard he sailed over the mountain opposite and disappeared. Heroic Lolly had saved the day!

Esme Cope (10)
Whirley Primary School, Macclesfield

Friends?

Once in the lost city of Atlantis there lived a cyclops eagle lion fish called Bonecrusher. Although he sounded violent, he was the friendliest creature. Swimming along towards the park, Bonecrusher got interrupted by an enemy, the Beast of the Coral. Everyone was scared of him. Ashamed, Bonecrusher ran away.

In the coral, someone was watching. They followed Bonecrusher into a secret place they had never been before, The Surface. That's when they revealed themselves. It was Teethy Tim from school and all his other friends. They told him that they were also scared of his enemy. "Friends, Bonecrusher?"

Isla Hogan (10)
Whirley Primary School, Macclesfield

Eye Girl Vs Professor Chicken Head

It was another mission for Eye Girl and her trusty assistant, Antenna Eye. Her eyes wiggled when there was danger around, so it was easy to know. Eye Girl loved being a superhero, even though it was tiring.

One day, Professor Chicken Head came for revenge. Eye Girl tried her hardest to defeat this demon of Eggabu! There was a *crash* and a *boom!* After, there was a *bang!*

The aliens of Spacealbania shouted, "Blob! Blob! Blob!" which means 'Eye Girl is our hero!' Meanwhile, Professor Chicken Head was locked up in a cell far, far away from Spacealbania itself.

Rosa Lamptey (7)
Whirley Primary School, Macclesfield

Escape To Sandwich Island

One lunchtime, Tim was just about to have lunch. Suddenly his sandwich jumped out of his lunchbox. Surprised, Tim looked at it in confusion.

"Rrrroarrr!" the sandwich cried. "You're not going to eat me!"

Tim, overcome by hunger, started grabbing for the sandwich. But, before he could get it, the sandwich zipped away and lifted the lids off the other lunchboxes, freeing the other sandwiches. It grabbed a fork from a nearby table and waved it at the hungry children.

The sandwiches made a run for it. "To the window!" they cried, and off into the sky they flew.

Matthew W (10)

Whirley Primary School, Macclesfield

The Mighty Crisp War

It was a normal day on Planet Frazzle when Bacon Frazzle Bob came along. Suddenly a rumble invaded Planet Frazzle. *Crash! Bang!* Bacon Bob looked around and found himself on Earth! He walked around and saw Hula Hoop Henry and Onion Ring Oliver! They approached him and started being mean to Bob. Without thinking, Bob made them disappear!

He suddenly heard a bang! Then the ground started to shake. *Flash! Bang!* The earth rumbled. Just then he found Hula Henry and Onion Oliver eating his secret stash of Frazzles. He immediately made them disappear. Bob didn't find them on Earth...

Millie Harrad
Whirley Primary School, Macclesfield

93

Octoforb And The Portal

Once upon a time, there lived three planets, Robot Planet, Octoforb Planet and Earth. Octoforb was an alien. He had three eyes and eight tentacles. Robots had invaded Octoforb's planet ever since it was created. So that meant robots had always been Octoforb's enemies.

A robot came to Octoforb's planet and opened up a portal to Earth. The robot pushed Octoforb in and he ended up on Earth. Once he got there, he was all alone and terrified until he met a very nice robot. Luckily, this robot opened another portal to Octoforb's planet. Suddenly, Octoforb had travelled home.

Isla Mather (8)
Whirley Primary School, Macclesfield

Luna's Self Discovery

On Planet Galar lives a little Galarine named Luna. Luna is vastly unique. While all his friends and family can fly, he can't. He is just plain old Luna. Everyone around him makes fun of him because he is different. Years pass while the ridicule continues. One day he finds himself fed up and frustrated. He closes his eyes desperately wishing he is somewhere else. *Pop!* Luna opens his eyes finding himself on a completely different planet. He explores! He is not an aviator, he is a teleporter! Suddenly a ferocious monster appears. Luna closes his eyes. *Pop!*

Rojvan Madiba Alagoz (10)
Whirley Primary School, Macclesfield

The Legendary Pokémon

Once, there was a powerful Pokémon called Mew Two. He was always in a bad mood with Ash and Goh for catching Pokémon. In the distance, Mew Two saw Ash and Goh. He knew Ash and Goh were going to try to catch him! Mew Two used 'aurasphere' but the attack missed and bounced behind Ash! The battle had begun!
Ash called out Lucario and ordered him to use 'double team', followed by 'steel beam'. Goh called out Cinderace and ordered him to use 'pyro ball'. Miraculously, they both landed a direct hit! Defeated, Mew Two flew away and escaped!

Fynn Prowting (7)
Whirley Primary School, Macclesfield

The Enchanted Valley

One day, Blossom the crystal cat was in her crystal cave. She was having fun with her twin sister Shimmer. They were looking at all the crystals: sapphire blue, emerald green, amber orange, ruby red. They gazed across the beautiful glimmering walls of the mystical cave. At the exact same moment, Scarlett was picking flowers from the field with her family.

"You can go off and play now!" her mum exclaimed.

Suddenly, the mouth of the cave was in front of her. She entered. Blossom was flying around, shooting crystals with her lasers. Scarlett looked up, astonished...

Eliza White (8)
Whirley Primary School, Macclesfield

The Terrifying Fright!

It was night-time and Lucy wished she could travel to Jupiter. She tightly closed her eyes, but when she opened them she was on planet Jupiter! "My wish came true!" Lucy cried.

Out of the distance came a three-eyed monster. "Argh! It's the scary Scoolips. I've read about this in a book," Lucy said. She tried and tried to kill it and eventually she did. When she killed it, she said, "Haha, I got you."

But after that, something strange happened. The ground began to rumble. Lucy thought it was an earthquake. The Scoolips was alive again!

Luke Pateman (7)
Whirley Primary School, Macclesfield

The Tickle Fight

There was a creature called Flougle. He was from Planet Narniers. His enemies were the aliens Harry, Barry and Larry.

One day, Flougle went to the Milky Way to get bananas, not knowing the aliens had come along with him. Flougle saw the aliens and told them off for following him.

He said, "Tickle fight. 1, 2, 3, tickle."

Flougle tickled the aliens' armpits, and they laughed so hard that a banana fell out of their eyes.

Flougle was excited to see his favourite food. They're now best buds, and when Flougle wants a banana, he tickles his friends.

Beth Shaul (7)
Whirley Primary School, Macclesfield

I Need A Friend

There is a small furry creature with big green fluorescent eyes. He may look cute, but inside he's fearsome like an angry gremlin.

He leaves his home planet in search of friends. In his wide and dangerous search, he finds a friendly family. His mischievous side comes out, so he decides to play some tricks on them. He steals their Christmas dinner and climbs up their Christmas tree until everything on the tree falls off, including the chocolates. He finds a little elf squirting soap around the house. He's just as mischievous as him. So they become best friends forever.

Sophie Arrowsmith (9)

Whirley Primary School, Macclesfield

Gobbleslime In A New World

Once upon a slime, Gobbleslime's friend Gotsy made up a competition because of his worst enemy. This was Slimsa, a bad-tempered minotaur alien who only cared about herself. The prize was that whoever won could give ten dares to the other. Gobbleslime's invention was a portal maker. Just then, Slimsa accidentally hit the red button and they went to the human world. Gobbleslime got some disguises while Slimsa tried to repair the portal maker. It took a very long time to repair the invention so Gobbleslime found the best food he could. Finally, they repaired it and flew back.

Amara Lamptey-Spencer (7)
Whirley Primary School, Macclesfield

The Earth Monster Meets Kitty

Kitty was stomping through the woods in a huff because her mum commanded Kitty to get the ingredients for the Christmas cookies. Kitty caught a glimpse of some squirrels leaping and hopping around so she chucked a few rounded pebbles at them as they got scared and froze in shock.

This is where the story gets weird. A mysterious, enchanting thing (the Earth Monster) came rolling up to her and bellowed, "That's not right!" and Kitty stumbled back as her body flooded with trepidation. From that day she knew never to be mean ever again and she kept her promise.

Erin Tench (9)
Whirley Primary School, Macclesfield

A Mysterious Time Traveller

One day, a mysterious time traveller travelled our world. On Friday, I was teleported to an unknown monster. He cackled. "Are you learning about the Stone Age?" said the monster.

I said, "Yes." And in the blink of an eye, I was back in the Stone Age. I was in a cave and saw lots of prehistoric pictures! I recognised the pictures and in our history lesson, our teacher gave us those pictures.

All of a sudden, I woke up. "I guess it was a dream," I said.

"You're late for break, now go for break," said the kind teacher.

Aiden Choi (7)
Whirley Primary School, Macclesfield

YoungWriters
Est. 1991

Snowa

The fluffy clouds hover above a magical land filled with magical creatures. It's a fluffy, bouncy land with clouds that look and taste of candyfloss. There lives a flying rainbow creature called Snowa, a magical Snowa, who is friends with everyone. She speaks all languages to not miss anyone out. Her days are like adventures, flying to all her friends, delivering bundles of happiness. Her favourite things to do are to fly from cloud to cloud and swing on strawberry laces, swim down the river of Vimto and most importantly have loads of fun in the magic world of Snowas!

Isabelle Hibberts (11)
Whirley Primary School, Macclesfield

Happy Heart

Planet Happy Heart gets a sense of sadness.
A girl is sad on Earth and needs some of Planet Happy Heart's magic.
Fizzbey is launched into space to find the girl on Earth. She sticks magic to her sticky pads. She finds Earth and uses her locator to find the girl.
Fizzbey hovers, the magic above her. A swoop of the wings and magic swirls around the girl.
The magic transforms the sadness into a smile and a happy heart.
Job done! Fizzbey gets her spacesuit on, clicks her jetpack and zooms through space to Planet Happy Heart. Mission accomplished.

Bella Heyes (8)

Whirley Primary School, Macclesfield

Moppy

Moppy's dancing like a slippery eel. Her body gets thinner and thinner and she turns into a slime snake. She stretches herself out like a rope to play skipping with her friends.

Stealthily, the coal leader from Coal Town disguises as a snake and slithers in to cause trouble. Using his body, he wraps around Moppy. They tumble around as Moppy tries to escape his black, sooty grip.

Suddenly, they fall into the slime cake, freeing Moppy who then turns into a boulder and crushes the coal leader.

Moppy saves the day. She then cleans up using her zooming mop.

Elijah Cockburn (7)

Whirley Primary School, Macclesfield

Mythical Milly's Magic Mayhem!

One sunny afternoon, on Planet Pixie, Mythical Milly sat swinging on her chair in her peaceful garden.

She was bored out of her mind so decided to get into some mischief!

With a flash of her horn, she turned the hose into another crazy creature. Meet Pippa Pipe!

Pippa and Milly giggled so loudly that they disturbed Bossy Billy next door, while he was relaxing in his mud crater. He leapt over the fence and shouted at Milly in his usual bossy way.

Milly cartwheeled over Billy to escape, but accidentally turned him into Kind Katie with her magical horn!

Olive McGillivray (8)

Whirley Primary School, Macclesfield

Roaming Ronnie

Roaming Ronnie is a brilliant little monster but he is made fun of because his head is inside his belly. As he was heading to school on Monday morning, someone called Bossy Bok came and loved to make fun of Roaming Ronnie and call him names. Until, one day, Roaming Ronnie was sitting on a beach all alone when someone came up to him and asked, "What's wrong?"

Roaming Ronnie told Precious Poppy everything that had been going on. Precious Poppy told Roaming Ronnie that he needed to tell the teacher, and so that's what happened. So everyone was happy.

Bella Hill (10)

Whirley Primary School, Macclesfield

The Football Match

It is the last few minutes of the most important football match ever at Planet Sportx. *The Stadium Of Hope is louder than ever,* thinks Pum-pum. His team, The Universal Dragons, are against The Firing Lions.

Pum-pum, in the last few minutes, fouls DJ! Is it a penalty? Yes, it's a penalty, but the question is, is it a red card? What! It's a yellow card; this is a problem. A big one.

DJ is stepping up to take his penalty. It's saved! Dragons are on the break; they cross. It's in, Pum-pum scores!

This is a miracle. They've won!

Gethin Herbert (9)
Whirley Primary School, Macclesfield

Untitled

One morning, an Aquadiablo called Eneya was swimming around the corner and saw many terrific, fascinating creatures. She was curious about a shadow, so she transformed into being invisible in case it was a stingray, blacktip shark or a lionfish.

As she crawled closer, she noticed it was also an Aquadiablo. Eneya immediately realised that it was scared, so she reassured her, and the other Aquadiablo said, "My name is Dolly."

The next morning, Eneya was swimming around but bumped into Dolly and said, "Hi" and they eventually became friends.

Molly Hogan (8)
Whirley Primary School, Macclesfield

Raffy And The Glompoms

Creatures from Lonton eat Glompoms to stop them from turning into strawberry jam. Glompom tastes cold and juicy. Lontons think it's like eating a banana, which they hate.

They soon missed them when the mean, spotty dragon destroyed them because of the smell. Brave King Raffy knew there were spare Glompoms on Neptune. As quick as a flash, Raffy jumped in his spaceship and set off to Neptune. When he got there, he shape-shifted into a tractor to collect as many as he could carry. As soon as he was full, he headed back to Lonton to save his creatures.

Evie Ashcroft (7)

Whirley Primary School, Macclesfield

Firework Freddy

Freddy erupted from the ground into the sky, and within a few seconds laser beams shot from his legs as he flew into the night. Freddy found himself travelling back to Earth, heading towards a playground. *Oh no!* Freddy thought as he crashed into the playground. *How on earth can I get myself out of here?* Freddy remembered that if he held his breath he would be able to use his magical powers to shoot into the sky.

29, 30, *pop!* Freedy soared into space. "Goodbye Bonfire Night," Freddy said to himself as he headed into the night.

Luca West (9)
Whirley Primary School, Macclesfield

Bad Habits

One day a monster from Mars came to Earth to get some food and bring it to his home planet. Nachoz, the deadly monster, used his tremendous sticky tentacles to catch the humans and travel back to Mars to eat them up and throw them into magical, terrifying space.

They were struggling. Surprisingly, one person had escaped the trap and was freed from the others. Nachoz saw them and fought them. It took lots of strength. A while later, the humans won the fight. "Wait," said one of the people, "how do we get down back home to planet Earth?"

Flynn Simister (8)
Whirley Primary School, Macclesfield

Fitness In His Galaxy Battles!

Fitness was the biggest and strongest monster in his city. He was fighting all the other monsters to be the strongest in the galaxy. Then he got through to the finals! He trained for weeks, months and years, and finally, his time for glory had come! When he came out of his fancy, lit-up tunnel, he heard thousands of fans screaming his name.
Soon after, they found themselves enemies. Then they jumped into the wrestling ring. Sweat was coming out quickly. Then the referee blew his loud whistle.
Their time was up and Fitness had won the World Title!

Charlie Macey (8)
Whirley Primary School, Macclesfield

Terry Saves Planet Hahoo

One day, a monster called Terry was born. No one liked him because he ate trash and smelt of trash. He really wished he had a friend.

At sunset, meteors made of rubbish attacked Planet Hahoo. Every monster on the planet ran for shelter, feeling very scared, apart from Terry. They thought it was the end of Planet Hahoo, but just then, Terry leapt into the air and ate all the trash balls.

The next day, the monsters realised that Terry had saved the planet. In the afternoon, everyone surprised Terry with a party. Now everyone was Terry's best friend.

Max Handley (7)
Whirley Primary School, Macclesfield

Mysteryfire

Once, in the Amazon rainforest, an expedition was happening. One explorer was desperate to find a new species. Far away still in the rainforest lay a creature. It had fangs, lots of legs and looked scary. The explorer found the creature and named it Mysterious.

When he got back the other explorers loaded their guns. Not to shoot him, but to shoot the creature. In a split second, the first bullet flew out of the gun. Everything was quiet, not because the Mysterious was dead but only to see all the explorers were dead apart from one. Mysterious killed them.

Arthur Gerrard (8)
Whirley Primary School, Macclesfield

Monster Town

Once there was a girl called Ava, who sat on her sofa watching TV one rainy afternoon. Suddenly, she pressed a button on her TV remote that she'd never seen before.

This opened a portal that sent her down, down, down into an unknown land. She saw weird creatures wandering around. This land was known as Monster Town.

Ava explored the town and found a small door. Behind it lived the friendliest monster in all of Monster Town. Ava and Om became best friends, sharing stories from both their lands.

After all the fun, Ava sadly had to go home!

Ava McClelland (7)
Whirley Primary School, Macclesfield

117

The Hero

Once, there was somebody called King Watermelon who went hiking with his family. Suddenly, there was an earthquake. King Watermelon was sent on a mission to win back the crystal that gave the land light and power because someone had stolen it. This is what made the earthquake. The King had to go and have a battle with the person who had stolen it, Melon Boy! Melon Boy was waiting with the power crystal. Out of nowhere, King Watermelon smashed the special hammer on Melon Boy and took back the crystal. Everyone cheered happily. King Watermelon saved the day!

Rory Owen (7)
Whirley Primary School, Macclesfield

The Brave Hearted Girl

One day, a little girl wandered through town, wishing someone would play with her. That day, she went to the Julia Donaldson Museum, and surprisingly, someone else was also there! Suddenly, a goblin popped out of nowhere, but she bombed him away. Then she looked behind her, and a shadow was coming at her! *What is it? Who is it? How did they get here? Where have they come from? How will I kill the shadow?* the girl wondered. "Run! Otherwise, this might not end well!" she said.

Just then, everyone needed to evacuate the building.

Orla Hill (8)

Whirley Primary School, Macclesfield

How The Monster Got Lightning Powers

Once upon a time, there lived a monster. He lived in a lightning world. But one day, the Lightning Monster said, "I want to go to the human world." But the Monster Mare said, "You cannot go to the human world because it is horrible."
Lightning Monster said, "How do you know it's horrible?"
The Mare said, "I went there once, but it was too much for monsters because my lightning powers absorbed all the energy in the town so I had to stay in the town."
"Okay," said Lightning Monster.

Ella Scragg (8)
Whirley Primary School, Macclesfield

Violet And The Big Fight

Once, Violet was walking through the woods and saw her enemy. The enemy asked, "Do you want a fight?"

Violet said, "Yes."

So, the next day, they had a giant fight. Violet chased after him and she hardly whacked him with her spiky tail. After, she chased and chased the big enemy spider. Finally, she won and she left for her monster den. She sat up on her purple bed and said, "I'm so, so proud of myself."

She went to sleep with a huge, fantastic smile. Off, then, she shut her eyes and fell asleep slowly.

Emily Stuart (8)
Whirley Primary School, Macclesfield

Bopstar Vs Harry

Bopstar is a reading monster who feeds on children that don't read enough. Can Harry survive Bopstar?

"Read or I feed!" chuckled Bopstar. As quickly as Harry could, he ran to the library. Bopstar wasn't far behind!

The library was just about to close. He had to run as fast as he could. He made it! Bopstar was stuck outside. Harry read a book, but Bopstar said it had to be 100 words!

So, Harry read a book with 100 words, but it took ages. Harry read it, but Bopstar broke in and shouted, "Good boy, Harry!"

Harry Kershaw (7)
Whirley Primary School, Macclesfield

The Atlantis Hero

Once upon a time, there was a mermaid who was living a normal life. One day, something unusual happened to Maria. She had to fight some bad guys!

They had stolen her dad's trident. She was fuming about her dad's trident. She lapped them, punched them and kicked them! Also, she double-kicked them.

When she got the trident back, she had to fight more bad guys. It was hard. When she fought them, she was exhausted after all the work.

She swam back to Atlantis to give the trident back to her father. She lived happily ever after.

Bobby Villers (7)
Whirley Primary School, Macclesfield

123

Elca

Elca was a monster who never felt accepted. All the monsters teased him for his claws. So one day Elca decided that he would leave his home planet and find a new one. His computer found a strange planet called Earth, so Elca landed his ship and set out to find friends.

One day he stumbled across a little girl called Ellie, who, like Elca, never felt accepted. So he asked her to be his friend and she almost immediately accepted despite his looks. So Elca and Ellie formed an immense bond despite being different. They lived happily ever after.

Isabelle Whitehead (10)
Whirley Primary School, Macclesfield

The Toasty Blizzard

Deep in the forest, in an enchanted cave, lived a cute little cotton monster called Cottoney. She was pink and fluffy and smelt beautiful. Her head and body were made of candyfloss and her hands and feet were made of marshmallows.

It was a cold winter's night and a blizzard was all around. Cottoney shivered and was as cold as ice. She collected some sticks and made a fire. The glowing fire made the cave toasty and warm but the cave wasn't the only thing toasty. Cottoney's hands and feet had melted! She was now just a fluff ball.

Isaac Jackson (8)
Whirley Primary School, Macclesfield

The Power Of Friendship

Mum was knitting a pink dragon, Clover, and a blue wolf, Fang. They were best friends and came alive at night. Zara, the dog, sniffed them out, dragging Clover into her blanket, but the dog's teeth caught his body. He was unravelling, and his stuffing was spilling out. To save Clover, he made a lasso from his unravelled wool and threw it to pull her to safety, but then he was too weak to move. *Friends help each other*, thought Clover and dragged Fang into Mum's knitting bag. Later, Mum fixed him! Zara smelled him again...

Isla Dougan (9)

Whirley Primary School, Macclesfield

Lupin's Hero

On Earth, there was a boy called Lupin. Lupin had a pet, quite a strange pet. It was a little crazy monster called Fang. Lupin brought Fang to school every day. There was one small problem—nobody liked Fang except Lupin.

One day when Lupin went to school, he brought his watch in. Bob, the school bully, and his monster Burt saw the new watch and hatched a plan to steal it. They had stolen from many other children before.

Fang searched hard, finding it hidden with lots of other stolen things, and from then on, he became a hero.

Max Joseph Brown (10)
Whirley Primary School, Macclesfield

Home

Gloop is a little blob who lives on Blopania. One day, he was bored. He looked left and right. Children blobs were playing. He saw a dark, blood-stopping cave. He slowly approached the cave. "Gurgle," he screamed as the cave closed behind him. He saw a different light. The light of Earth! He got to work quickly. He dashed for metal, and shape-shifted on the way! He went to a garage and got to work and built a... rocket! But humans dashed in to attack, but he was already gone. In a hurry, he ran home and never left again.

Ted Bailey (8)
Whirley Primary School, Macclesfield

The Unhappy Mr Hairy

Nora and Eve were sitting on their beds. Nora was happily gaming on her console when suddenly a cloud of blue smoke appeared in front of her and her console vanished into thin air. Eve was enjoying reading her new book when a cloud of blue smoke appeared in front of her and her book disappeared! This made them both confused and upset.

Then they saw a big, brown, hairy creature. It grew bigger until it was the size of the country. Then everyone became upset and angry, so they turned against Mr Hairy and defeated him. Everyone was happy!

Lilliana Millward (10)
Whirley Primary School, Macclesfield

Odd Teddy

Once upon a time, a cute bear called Joff turned invisible. It was incredible because he absolutely hated gorillas and snakes. However, he lived in the jungle, so he bumped into them a lot!
One day, he found an odd-looking banana that looked so odd, he ate it. This was a bad idea because he turned mystical and evil. He caused chaos everywhere. He turned into a six-eyed monster.
After a while, he gave in and felt sick. He lay down and fell asleep. Suddenly, he threw up. He felt normal, safe, warm and the same old teddy bear.

Coen Beech (9)

Whirley Primary School, Macclesfield

Squirkey The Turkey Vs Kricken The Chicken

After waking up, Squirkey looked around curiously. This wasn't where he'd fallen asleep. He wandered for ages till he saw something odd. Another one like him, yet he had a chicken body and was bullying some dogs. He was using his sticky feet to stick to a building and laughing at them.

He had to stop them so he went and grabbed the chicken and pulled him off the wall! The dogs cheered as he pulled him around the garden, going faster and faster till he was a blur. Then he released the chicken and launched him in the air.

Paddy Considine (10)
Whirley Primary School, Macclesfield

Fishing Trip

Sitting in my boat on the peaceful lake, my fishing rod suddenly spun as fast as Usain Bolt! Speedily, the fishing line came to a halt. On the end of the line was a monster-like creature. Long arms, four fingers, one big eye, a frowning mouth and a fifteen-feet long tail.

It was so hard to reel the monster in. It nearly broke the fishing rod. My dad had to help pull the monster in. Luckily, we had super strength together. We felt like trophy winners, triumphing together. We love our fishing trips together. We called it Doomboo.

Harry Hibberts (9)
Whirley Primary School, Macclesfield

Fireball

Once there was a gentle dragon with knife-like teeth. Her dream was to go to the real world. She packed her bags and left her dreamy land.
As she arrived, the police saw her and she almost floated into the water. Then the wanted signs went up. She got out of the water and bumped into a girl who was fascinated! Then the dragon's parents arrived to take her home but the little girl wanted her to stay. She went home, promising the girl she'd come back.
Two years later the dragon came back and stayed for a whole year.

Sadie Watkins (8)
Whirley Primary School, Macclesfield

The Rocky Mountain

"The rules are simple. We all sit around the fire and tell myths but if you get scared and run away, you are out! Who wants to go first?" explained Emma.
"Me, me, I want to go first," cried Luna.
"Ready to be scared? The Myth Of The Rocky Mountain. People say if you go to the Rocky Mountain at night, you'll see-"
"Ahh!" screamed Layla.
"I'm not even at the good part yet!" moaned Luna. Little did she know, there was a hideous creature emerging behind her!

Nola Campbell (10)
Whirley Primary School, Macclesfield

The Cloud Demon

One day, Elephant Airlines took off from Tiger Airport to fly to Lionty. Soon after they got off the runway, they ran into a petrifying storm that almost threw the plane upside down. They spotted teeth and flew away before spotting a hand trying to grab them. Next, an eye the size of a house was staring at them. Then they escaped!
Relieved, the pilot took a nap, but when he awoke he was back in the storm, flying around spikes as sharp as the sharpest knives that had to have perfection to fly through. What was going to happen?

Oliver Pateman (10)
Whirley Primary School, Macclesfield

The War

Once upon a time, there were ten Nacume fruits but there were hundreds of Space Crawlers. It was on planet BO-258-01. It was called Super Saturn. They were in a war. The Space Crawlers kept eating the Nacume fruits and stood no chance. But then, far far away was the queen. She bred for years and years and had thousands of Nacume fruits.

Then they all got sent to fight... After all of the severe war, there were no living Space Crawlers on the battlefield. They had won the war! This story was meant for you to learn resilience.

Jude Charnock (8)
Whirley Primary School, Macclesfield

The Journey Of Life

In the galactic world of Pom, Princess Pom Pom was looking for her friend to tell her some news. She was so excited to tell her about the five ingredients. But she did not know that the trogs were after it too.

As she set off, on her journey, she met one person from each team, including the trogs. She battled for each ingredient. The princess got to the final battle - she had to battle the trogs! In the end, she won.

When she arrived home, she created the potion. From the smoke, rose the crystal of colour. Bounce!

Eliza Utteridge (8)
Whirley Primary School, Macclesfield

137

Late For School

One day, Tappy woke up to an alarming thought. His thought was, *what time is it? What if I'm late for school?* He grabbed his school bag with a tight clench, rushing towards the door. He barged out and ran to school.

As he finally reached school, he put his bag away and headed to class, but only just now he realised he was the only one roaming the school halls. He checked his watch to see the time and to his surprise, it was 9:30! Now he was running.

He sat down in his seat. Let's get to work!

Ellie Norbury (9)
Whirley Primary School, Macclesfield

Never Trust Byron

Byron is my name and I am playing a big game. Fursball! I always challenged everyone and I never lost. This was until I met Freddie. The monster with the biggest heart in the world. He beat me at football but he actually cheated. After that game, I got so angry that I turned into the scariest monster in the world. Everyone hated me.
One day when I was scaring everyone I came across Freddie, and he hugged me. I screamed so loudly that even I found it annoying! I had no more anger and me and Freddie became friends.

Oscar Furness (11)
Whirley Primary School, Macclesfield

Crazy Creatures Cup Final

Today, you crazy fans, we have an exciting day at the Long-Legged Football Academy. Are you ready for the Crazy Creature Cup Final, where Leech United play the Burn Boys?

The whistle goes at Stinky Stadium and Haaland the Hot Head gets the ball and passes to De Bruyne the Burning Ball. He shoots and he misses. Lawraldo gets the ball and dribbles with all his legs to the goal and scores with a scorpion kick.

The final whistle blows and Leech United win the Crazy Creature Cup Final and are crowned champions!

Lawrence Litherland (8)

Whirley Primary School, Macclesfield

Crocophant

My monster is called Crocophant and he is seven years old. He is a boy and he is a carnivore. He has sharp teeth. He was born on Wednesday 29th November 2016, and it is his birthday. His favourite food is a big wild boar!

Today, he had a nasty surprise. Chomping into his dinner, he lost a tooth. It hurt so much he cried. Luku, his best friend in the world, was at the dentist. Using specialist glue, he stuck it back together.

He was happy. He invited his friend for dinner. They had the best time ever.

Alfie Sherratt (7)
Whirley Primary School, Macclesfield

The Good And The Bad

One day, a creature was lurking about when she heard her name. "Star," shouted a familiar voice. Star felt something bad was about to happen. "Star, the bad monsters have passed through the barrier." Mist was trembling from head to toe. Star shuddered. This could only mean one thing. She had to go.

Mist and Star stood side by side. As the barrier opened, the monster in front of them said, "Friends?"

What have we been worried for? they both thought. Then, it smiled!

Eve Lewis (9)

Whirley Primary School, Macclesfield

Beastly Bolognese

One day, deep, deep down under, in a place called Bob's Bolognese, there was a secret lab that belonged to the beast, which was created. Bob, who owned the restaurant, made him help with making food to serve. The first time he made it, he was three months old, and he wasn't very good. As time slowly went on and the beast turned 1, 5, 10, 15, and then when it was 20, he had mastered the dish. Soon, he helped serve with Bob. So, Bob died of old age, and the beast renamed it and made the dish himself!

Callum Casey (10)
Whirley Primary School, Macclesfield

Stinky Bob Comes To Earth

Stinky Bob came to town. He imagined it to be like Crazy Creature Town, but there was no place to stay, and there were no monsters to play with. However, he thought that all the monsters were just secretly hiding.

The next day, he went to the nearest school, and it was not what he imagined it to be like. On the walls were beautiful displays rather than the insane random walls he was used to, but then he noticed a girl looking excitedly at him. He asked her name; it was Bella, and they became best friends.

Bella Burrows-Jarvis (9)
Whirley Primary School, Macclesfield

The Crazy Kittens!

One day the crazy kittens woke up. Before they even opened their eyes, they started knocking into chairs. They jumped on the table and ate the food on the table!

The kittens were called Oreo, Vinnie and Rodney. At the start of the day, they charged up the stairs and jumped on the beds like they owned the place. They galloped down the stairs like a herd of elephants.

After eating the food, they searched around the house. They finally fell asleep but an hour later, there'll be more crazy kittens!

Lola Rowson (7)
Whirley Primary School, Macclesfield

145

Terror In The Park

It was a beautiful day in Balloonville, so Balloon Man went for a walk in the newest park on Earth. But he encountered one of his natural enemies—children! As he started to walk away from the little monsters, they spotted him and started to chase him.

He hid under a bridge, and as soon as he thought he was safe, a child popped from behind him. Luckily, at that moment, a gust of wind lifted him into the air, and he flew higher and higher, until suddenly, he stopped flying and landed in a nursery!

Callie Davies (10)
Whirley Primary School, Macclesfield

How Mars Began

One night Bogtrotter was just about to go to bed, but he suddenly got a shock in his right arm. He didn't think anything of it and went to bed.

When he woke up, he saw a portal at the end of his bed and almost immediately went in it. The moment he got in, nothing was there. He realised he had superpowers and created a new world over the past 10,000 years.

When he finally finished, he brought all of the monsters that were on Earth to Mars. As the years pass he makes life better for monsters.

Lucas Scott (11)
Whirley Primary School, Macclesfield

An Unexpected Situation

Today was the big day. Our team made it to the finals and we were facing a really strong opponent.

The game started. It was 2-0 at half-time but we brought it back to 2-2. Suddenly, my thought became real! *I am Madfoot*, explained the thought. *My enemies are the goalkeepers. Watch this shot...* I slammed the ball and it went so high. It went higher than the stadium. But all of a sudden, the ball came down so fast that it bounced over the keeper and went in and my team won the finals.

Anson Choi (10)
Whirley Primary School, Macclesfield

The Human Slayer

Once upon a time, a boy went into the Forbidden Forest until he got lost. He was all alone with no food or water. He had to find a home.

Eventually, he found a cave. As he went in deeper and deeper, a mythical creature came out of nowhere and bit him! Day after day, he became more and more evil and scarier. Whoever went in, never came out.

A sheriff went to check it out. He saw blood everywhere. He saw human remains like a heart. He heard a growl that got closer and closer. He started running.

Charles Thomas (8)
Whirley Primary School, Macclesfield

The Mystery Destiny

On Rainbow Mist Island, it was a misty, miserable morning because a pony called Comet had lost her sister Destiny. So, she went for a nap and in a vision, she saw an old, wise horse and decided to wake up and find her. Soon, she found the horse and asked if she could tell him where she could find the slide to the human world. She scoured the beach for many days and soon found the slide to the human world. She entered the human world and after a while, she found a magical, beautiful but dark, evil horse.

Matilda Naughton (8)
Whirley Primary School, Macclesfield

Fire And Water

One day, Fire was walking past the town when out of nowhere came King Water, ruler of the land. Fire was very afraid of him.

Suddenly the alarm went off and it was a child learning to swim, and they needed someone who was willing to help her. Ferocious Fire put his hand up then King Water put his hand up, so they both started to help the little girl. But King Water made it there first so they raced each other to the little girl and helped her back to Mars. They became friends and the job was done.

Mia Scragg (10)
Whirley Primary School, Macclesfield

151

Anyone Can Be Friends

One day, Rainbow Cloud was bored. She tried to ask someone to play but they said no. So, she asked her friends to come to her den. But they still said no. So she walked back to her house and onto her bed and saw a button. So she pressed it. A wormhole appeared! She stood up and she jumped into it.

When she got in, a girl was waiting at the other end. She said, "Hello." They curiously looked at her and asked, "Do you want to play?" So that is what they did! Then, she went home.

Niamh Lee (8)
Whirley Primary School, Macclesfield

The Argonitha

One eerie night, I heard a noise from a colossal pit in the ground. Something unsettling was going through my heart as I jumped into the bottomless pit. Was this the end?
Suddenly, a grim shadow appeared as if it was behind me and it faded away. Did I dare to look behind me? An ear-splitting roar shook me. Before I even got a chance to make my decision, a shadow appeared on the wet soil. My hands vibrated as I could barely move. Fear gripped my heart. Was this the end of my amazing life?

Jack Robson (8)
Whirley Primary School, Macclesfield

Peace Broken But Not Broken

On Earth it was peaceful as Bull was relaxing; nothing was wrong, everything was fine. Suddenly, Franky Boomer came down to Earth and destroyed a really tiny village. The village people called the police who then called Bull. Straight after, Bullgaria got his cape, put it on then flew to the tiny village. As he was flying he shot some laser balls from his four cannons. It hit him so he was confused. When he was not looking Bull came from the air and hit him on the face then he left. Job done!

Ronnie Tsang (9)
Whirley Primary School, Macclesfield

Alexander And Mr Man

One day at Boggle Land, Alexander was minding his own business and Mr Man threw a giddle at him. "Who was that?" he said.
"Me!"
So Alexander and Mr Man had a battle. Alexander won and threw Mr Man to the land of rubbish which was filled with rubbish.
Mr Man had an idea, he was going to buy a spaceship. But Alexander knew that he was going to be defeated so he decided to hide in the snoggle and scare Mr Man, so he hid and scared Mr Man to Banana Land.

Lewis Furness (9)
Whirley Primary School, Macclesfield

155

My Crazy Creature

The Whechidigsanbicholboo was a smart, kind and little creature. It took on every challenge with a smile on its face, apart from one thing, swimming. Although it tried and tried, it just couldn't.
Until one day... thinking outside the box, it started using its wheel. The Whechidigsanbicholboo had perfected it!
It had come. The day it would compete. Three, two, one! *Go!* It started off slowly but it was picking up the pace. 4th, 3rd, 2nd, 1st. It had done it.

Edwin Williams-Higuchi (10)
Whirley Primary School, Macclesfield

Untitled

Once upon a time, there lived a monster called Crazy and he loved to play. But there were two other monsters. Their names were Red and Green. They were mean to Crazy because his name was Crazy. But Crazy isn't crazy. He is smart, like an owl.

He found out that Green and Red were leaving because they said they were too smart to be here. They were packing up. It was the best day ever. Then, they got in their monster truck and left. They lived happily ever after.

Freddie Blackburn (8)

Whirley Primary School, Macclesfield

Untitled

Once upon a time, in a faraway land lived what looked like an ordinary man. He was anything but when the sun came down and the moon rose; he became the god of poachers with scissory fangs, electric blue hair and the neatest suit and tie you'd ever see. Along with those strange looks he had a unique ability called supervision.

One night, while hunting someone took his kill. Since nobody had the guts to do it before he went into a ballistic rage over and over again.

Ashley Foster (10)
Whirley Primary School, Macclesfield

War As A Crisp

One day, there was a crisp called Bacon Frazzle Man. He was very mysterious. He had an enemy called Cheese and Onion Chad. He had many more, but Cheese and Onion Chad stood out the most.
Suddenly, Bacon Frazzle Man got a knock on his door. It was the queen asking him to go to the war. He was in shock but he still said yes. So he got his gear and then went. There were loads of other crisps in the war. He was about to get shot, but what happened to him...?

Annabel Jones (10)
Whirley Primary School, Macclesfield

Whirly

Bo was a fluffy, courageous monster and he lived on a planet called Zophat. One day Zog was being mean to him. Zog rammed into Bo and hurt him badly. This made him angry and he decided to get even! He jumped up and down to make Zog dizzy so that he could ram him back. Bo jumped so high that he landed heavily on Zog and broke his ankle. It made Bo realise that if someone hurts you, you don't hurt them back. You should tell someone you trust.

Shea Raylance (8)
Whirley Primary School, Macclesfield

A Crazy Creature's Life

In Never-Ending Land, a creature called Bloop was at school, but he was getting bullied by another creature called Splat. Bloop didn't really care about it, but he thought, *what is space?*
I thought he must be joking, but he truly wanted to know. Bloop was going to go in a rocket to space, but little did he know that Splat was going too. Bloop didn't know until they took off. Splat surprised him. Bloop wasn't happy.

Poppy Barnes (9)
Whirley Primary School, Macclesfield

Bob The Plumber

One day, Bob was checking out a known planet. This was his first assignment so he must not screw up. The planet he was checking was Planet Fagling. So he was going to get the space taxi. As he went, he felt hungry, so he went to the agency as soon as he landed. He went to Miss Maclean's house to check her bathroom. He did as soon as he got there. He went to the bathroom so he checked every inch. He was very nosy indeed.

Matthew Cain (9)
Whirley Primary School, Macclesfield

The Season To Hunt

It is the day before Halloween. Dark Cloak is super excited because he thinks he will get loads and loads of kills. He does not know that it is Covid so everybody is going to stay home.

The next day he is so excited he waits all day but at the end of the day, he sees that no one is in a costume. He realises that it is Covid and he is really sad.

He cries before he goes home and night turns to the morning.

Jacob Morton-Collings (8)
Whirley Primary School, Macclesfield

The Never Yeti

Once upon a time, a never-fluffy yeti lived on a planet called Spumnayo, next to Jupiter. Suddenly, he sneezed and flew all the way back down to Earth. He went to the local shop, and everyone was screaming and shouting at him, so he left the shop and was lonely.

Suddenly, a pack of cute dogs surrounded him. The dogs were magical; they could talk to him, and he finally found a ton of friends.

Lucas Olive (9)
Whirley Primary School, Macclesfield

The Monster That Went To School

Once there was a monster called Purp. Purp wanted to go to school. He went to school for a day. He was on his way, when he saw more monsters going to school.

He finally got to school and had the best time of his life, so he went again and again until he couldn't. Then he went to college and university.

Savannah Woodward (9)

Whirley Primary School, Macclesfield

YOUNG WRITERS INFORMATION

We hope you have enjoyed reading this book – and that you will continue to in the coming years.

If you're a young writer who enjoys reading and creative writing, or the parent of an enthusiastic poet or story writer, do visit our website **www.youngwriters.co.uk**. Here you will find free competitions, workshops and games, as well as recommended reads, a poetry glossary and our blog.

If you would like to order further copies of this book, or any of our other titles, then please give us a call or visit **www.youngwriters.co.uk**.

Young Writers
Remus House
Coltsfoot Drive
Peterborough
PE2 9BF
(01733) 890066
info@youngwriters.co.uk

Scan me to watch the Crazy Creatures video!

 YoungWritersUK   **YoungWritersCW**

 youngwriterscw   **youngwriterscw**